Toy's

For my sister,
Jessie

First published 2002 by Walker Books Ltd
87 Vauxhall Walk, London SE11 5HJ

10 9 8 7 6 5 4 3 2 1

© 2002 Tor Freeman

This book has been typeset
in OPTI Typewriter Special

Printed in China

British Library Cataloguing
in Publication Data: a catalogue record
for this book is available from
the British Library

ISBN 0-7445-7548-6

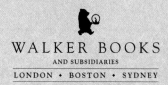

WALKER BOOKS
AND SUBSIDIARIES
LONDON · BOSTON · SYDNEY

RAH!

Tor Freeman

Last night,
Mum read Lotte
a story about
animals from her
favourite book.

When Lotte woke
up this morning,
she was a lion.

Lotte went
downstairs
and Mum said,
"Good morning."

"Lions don't say good morning,
RAH!" Lotte said.

Next, when Mum
was sewing,

Lotte
turned into
a monkey.

Mum said, "Be careful not to trip over."
"Monkeys don't trip over,
    RAH!" Lotte said.

Then Mum and
Lotte played
hide-and-seek.
Lotte was an
elephant.

"Here I come!"
called Mum.

She couldn't
find Lotte
anywhere.

Lotte jumped out.
"RAH!" she said.

After lunch
Mum had some
jobs to do.
Lotte was
a bear.

The bear and Mum watered
the plants together.

The bear and
Mum built a
tower together.

Mum said,
"Not too high
or it'll fall."

RAH!

"No it won't,
RAH!"
Lotte said.

But it did.

By supper-time Lotte was a crocodile.
"Eat up your vegetables," said Mum.

"Crocodiles don't like vegetables,
    RAH!" Lotte said.

After supper,
Lotte was still
a crocodile.

"Bedtime, Lotte,"
Mum said.
"Shall I carry
you upstairs?"

"I'm not Lotte! I'm a
crocodile," Lotte said.
"And crocodiles don't
like being carried
upstairs, RAH!"

RAH!

"Oh!" said Mum, "I'm not sure
I like crocodiles."

The crocodile
sat alone at the
bottom of the stairs.

Mum came and sat beside her.
"Crocodiles don't like being
carried upstairs," Mum said.
"But I know someone who does.
Do you?"

"I think I do,"
said the crocodile...

Mum hugged
Lotte and
carried her
upstairs.

Lotte put on
her pyjamas
by herself.

"I'm glad you're
Lotte again,"
Mum said.

Then she read Lotte a story
about a little penguin.
Mum kissed Lotte goodnight.
"Sweet dreams, Lotte," she said.

"RAH!" said the little penguin ...

and she went to sleep.